ARROWOOD BOOKS, INC.
SANTA MONICA, CA

First Edition

ARROWOOD BOOKS, INC.
2118 WILSHIRE BLVD., SUITE 271
SANTA MONICA, CALIFORNIA 90403-5784
UNITED STATES OF AMERICA
WWW.ARROWOODBOOKS.COM

Design & Layout by Mike McCullen
Nest Illustration by Scott Cattanach
Color Photography by Richard Hines

Printed in Hong Kong by Toppan Printing Co.

10 9 8 7 6 5 4 3 2 1

Publisher's Cataloging-in-Publication Data

Briggs, Virginia Morris

The nest / Virginia Morris Briggs. – 1st ed.
p. cm.
ISBN: 0-9674861-0-6

1. Birds--Fiction. 2. Spiritual life--Fiction
I. Title

PS3552.R4559N47 2000 813.6
QBI00-333

For The Nurturers

We all have a nest . . .
a special place of refuge

The moon has awakened and assembled the stars. Dulcet sounds of tiny bells waft on gentle, fragrant air. Softly clinging to the end of a shimmering silver string, a drop of starlit dew tranquilly descends toward Earth. Enshrined within it, this seed of a new soul, having no memory of the past, will make only new choices. Sparkling with unlimited potential, its destiny now below, this shining drop of dew from heaven above is about to become one with a small, warm, glossy blue egg, now waiting in the twig, cup-shaped nest of an American Robin.

THE ROBIN

. . . herald of spring

Where the center of a New England city has softened to houses with lawns, gardens, and little woods with stands of sugar maples, shagbark hickories, and white pines, the spring nesting season is under way.

The early-morning dew moistens the trees and bonnets the buds of the yellow daffodils as a mother-to-be American Robin perfectly centers the first of a clutch of three blue glossy eggs in her cup-shaped nest. The twig edifice straddles a high limb of an old Oak tree that stands behind a gray clapboard house with black shutters and white trim.

At daybreak on the following consecutive days, she will add two more Robin's blue eggs to her well-constructed nest.

Three weeks earlier, her mate, a large American Robin with a slate-gray back, blackish tail and head, white-streaked throat, and a brick-red breast, had perched high atop the old Oak, his yellow bill opened wide, pouring forth his full-throated, melodious song – a prerogative of male robins only.

He vigorously defended his exclusive territory – the woods behind the house, the owner's well-tended, partially-blooming flower garden, a potting shed, and a small, newly-planted herb and vegetable garden. Included in his domain was the long gravel driveway from the main road in front of the house, which ran past arbored grapevines not yet in leaf to the back of the modest brick-chimneyed dwelling. Here a young green lawn extended from the back porch to the nesting Oak, under which stood an oversized birdbath, two hanging feeders for small perching birds, and an elevated wooden feeding platform.

As regularly as the light of a new day, a gray-haired human being, nature's only other two-legged creature, dressed in white and wearing a khaki field jacket, would appear at the back porch door.

A true nurturer and protector of her feathered friends, this sometimes binocular-eyed old woman walked briskly to the potting shed and soon emerged with a basket full of tiny seeds for the hanging feeders, suet in small net bags for easy access by downy Woodpeckers and chickadees, apples and raisins for robins, and cracked corn and sunflowers for the birds that fed at the platform feeder – cardinals, doves, and Dark-eyed Juncos.

She knew the importance of feeding the birds year round. Providing food, especially in the springtime, allowed them to spend more time on the nest and for parenting their young. Teaching their fledglings how to take seeds from the hanging tubular feeders was another benefit. And the rest of the year, migrant birds that the old woman might not otherwise see would be more likely to visit her backyard for food.

She filled the birdbath with fresh water from the garden hose, stood silently listening for a while, and then went back into her house.

After watching this morning ritual, the expectant Robin remembered that fourteen days had passed since she had first placed her warm body over her eggs and the incubation of the embryos, carrying the ancient genetic code of the parents, had begun.

As she crouched low on her nest she felt a faint call from the first-laid egg, and her large black eyes reflected a low-slanted ray of morning sun filtering through the Oak leaves. I'll name my first-born Robin Ray, she thought, hearing the second small peep. Invisibly, life had begun within the blue egg cradle.

As if performing a ritual it had practiced a thousand times before, the baby chick, still within, rhythmically moved her tiny head up and down in a continuous motion.

The chick was allowing her egg tooth, a saw-like protuberance on her beak, to perform its one-time function, setting her free from her yoke-nourished shelter.

From inside their eggs, two other chicks soon performed the same process, producing Robin Ray's brothers. Since they are altricial chicks, born without feathers and totally dependent on their parents for survival, the tiny new birds would be cared for by the mother Robin and her mate until they could fly on their own. Before the weather turned cold she would move on to build another nest, leaving her mate to complete the nurturing and pass on his knowledge to them.

During these first few weeks, part of the information gained by young males is learning to sing the proper song. Their brains incorporate accurate records of their fathers' songs, allowing the birds to perfectly reproduce them the following spring when they begin their own mating and nesting. Or the songs of other male neighbors in their territory are copied, so that when they return to their area they can sing the songs that are common to it. In this way they are not considered outsiders who would be harassed by other robins.

For the nestlings, nature's cycles of courtship, egg-laying, brooding, fledging, and migration would move at a highly accelerated pace that allotted an average one-and-a-half-year life span, energized by a heart that would beat nearly 600 times a minute.

As new members of the Thrush family, the three baby robins had joined the more than 9000 living bird species.

Known as the American Robin, one of the 800 North American species, including migrants, they would be part of the Order Passeriformes, which contains more than half of the avian species. As Passerines, the perching birds, "songbirds" noted for their ability to sing, they were about to be assigned their seats in the world chorus.

Since a bird with ancient wings – *archaeopteryx* – had first taken its faltering flight from the trees surrounding the lagoons and shallow seas of southern Jurassic Germany, 150 million years of programmed, behavioral instinct had been passed on, bird to bird, embryo to embryo, egg to egg. Land-bound no more, for the first time these feathered ancestors had been free to oppose the will of gravity and fly up to see more than any other creature had ever been able to observe before.

As a late afternoon breeze tinkled the wind chimes on the back porch of the house below, mother Robin joyfully recalled the morning sun that had attended the birth of her first-born. "Robin Ray – it's a perfect name for her!" she whispered.

Father Robin, already in flight gathering food to meet the staggering needs of his new family, would insist on naming the boys.

TAKING WING

2

. . . it's a big world

The twelve-to-fifteen-day fledging period had not gone well. The mother Robin's mate was not doing his part, disappearing in the woods for long periods of time and having little to say when he returned.

Robin Ray's brothers made fun of the fact that her egg tooth had not fallen off as theirs had, but despite their taunts she was developing strong legs to stand up to compete with them for food.

Late one afternoon, when her mother had left the nest for a brief respite, Robin Ray could hear both her parents strenuously arguing by the birdbath, below. After the noisy fight they returned to the nest. Her mother was extremely agitated and missing several head feathers.

"If you won't remove that ugly bump on her bill, I will!" cried her father. He was pointing his head toward Robin Ray.

Her frightened mother pleaded with him. "I'm sure that her egg tooth will come off in its right time. Please, please, let's wait!"

Without warning, with one swift thrust of his yellow beak, her infuriated father tore the egg tooth from her tiny bill, almost lifting her out of the nest.

"Now is the right time!" he said angrily. He flew off without a backward glance and they could see him heading rapidly towards the darkening woods.

Terrified at the sudden attack, Robin Ray saw her mother, who had tried to protect her, flung backwards on the nest. Without a sound, mother Robin gathered her nestlings under her wings and prepared for the long night. When morning came, her father had not returned. Her mother's repeated, insistent call note did not bring a response.

In the days that followed, mother Robin did the best she could, feeding the nestlings herself and teaching them all that she knew. Her stance was erect and her head high, but Robin Ray saw that her bright black eyes had lost their luster and that she was very weary.

Shortly after the three nestlings got their wings, Robin Ray's brothers found her near the potting shed and told her they were leaving. Robin Ray began to protest, but, eager to find new territories, the two young birds took flight and disappeared over a stand of sugar maples.

She flew quickly to tell her mother, but did not find her at the nest. Robin Ray searched for hours, but there was no sign of her.

Then, as she was returning, exhausted, to the old Oak, Robin Ray saw the familiar white-clad human being. She was crouching near the birdbath, starting to cover the mother bird's still body with moist earth. Solemnly, the bird lover finished the task and placed a purple lilac on top of the small, fresh mound. She bowed her head for a moment and then walked slowly into her house.

Robin Ray, filled with overwhelming rage, vowed never to forgive her father. "Never . . . ever, ever!" she cried aloud.

Overcome with grief, she stared transfixed at her mother's empty nest. It was now the sole memento of the connection between parent and young, a moment that seemed to have been as fleeting as springtime.

Her heart pumped rapidly under her brown and yellow spotted breast. For the first time in her life, Robin Ray was completely alone.

How will I ever find my way? she thought. She trembled with fear.

SHARP-SHINNED HAWK

3

. . . red in beak and claw

A few weeks later, when her grief was subsiding, Robin Ray decided that she would go to the cliffs to observe and to see what she could learn from the high-flying, powerful birds of prey, the hawks, eagles, and falcons.

Hiding herself atop a tall conifer, she spied a large eagle commanding a precipice on the rocks above. With a sharp eye, he surveyed all that lay below.

The sky was darkening with storm clouds and a gaunt Sharp-shinned Hawk was heading for its stick nest in a nearby pine tree. Robin Ray would have to be cautious! She had heard that hawks time the laying of their eggs so that after two months of training, the fully-fledged young leave their nest to sharpen their hunting skills on fledgling songbirds.

As the sky continued to darken, her secret watch continued. She saw the two falcons, a parent and a newly-fledged offspring, practice diving, gliding, and turning. The father was teaching him the prerequisites for survival.

Her admiration mixed with envy as, over and over again, she watched the obedient young falcon perfecting his dives and then sharply tilting his wings to pull out and up from his rapid descent.

A sudden clap of thunder flushed two migrant Red-winged Blackbirds upward from the trees in confused flight, directly into the path of the gliding falcons.

Without changing his forward motion a beat, the experienced falcon parent extended his taloned feet and grabbed one of the hapless birds.

A quick command to his student and the fledgling tried to turn upside down and fly on his back to receive the struggling prey. He was not quick enough nor practiced enough for the new task, and the Blackbird, torn feathers now floating free, fell toward the treetops.

The lone eagle had been observing and now joined the fray, as did the old Sharp-shinned Hawk, all fighting claw to claw and beak to beak, their bodies swirling in air. The rain began to fall in hard drops, and Robin Ray watched the birds, now on the ground, as they fought over the dead Blackbird.

In the excitement, she did not see the old Hawk return to her stick nest until she heard a low, mournful cry. She carefully approached the nest and saw a scrawny bird with dull talons, crooked beak, and a hanging broken wing – a tattered Hawk, spent by age and effort.

Only half-seeing through her pain and failing eyesight, she looked at Robin Ray with somber eyes. "Luz's wings are no longer wings to fly. I am old," she said. "Nothing stays the same, life is not all soaring and flying free, but short, uncertain, and full of perils. Oh, that we had many lifetimes!" she added weakly. Her eyes grew cloudy.

Robin Ray did not know what to say or what to do. She thought of her mother.

"You are not a raptor, you are a young songbird!" the old Hawk said. "Prepare yourself, now, for the fever and fret of this world and for the time the raven will try to eat your eyes out!"

Robin Ray shivered.

Luz, the life force draining from her feathered body, struggled to her feet. The sun had reappeared, and the rain was softening; only the sound of distant thunder rumbled through the trees.

"Do you see the vast flocks forming on the mountain?" Luz asked, her voice strengthening, her eyes staring at a faraway mountain, now ever-so-faintly evident through the clouds. "There are thousands of shimmering birds! Look! Look how bright their feathers are!"

Robin Ray strained her eyes toward the mountain. She could see no birds, no bright flocks, only a swirling screen of rapidly moving clouds and a momentary glimpse of what appeared to be its smooth dome, splashed with colors from a fleeting rainbow.

Robin Ray watched, stunned, as the old Hawk lifted from her nest in a newly-found surge of power, glided upwards, let out a piercing cry, and fell silently to earth.

The old Hawk seemed so certain that there were flocks of birds on the mountain, thought Robin Ray. She was glad she had not answered Luz when she asked if she had seen them too.

Thankful for the steady, stable beat of her heart, Robin Ray was glad to be flying home to her own safe territory.

Just before she was to emerge from the woodlands, she spotted a fast-moving falcon headed directly for her, its sharp talons extended. With only seconds to spare before the strike, she tilted her wings at a severe angle and made an abrupt, upward turn. The move totally confused the swift falcon, who flew on through the trees with only her single tail feather in his talons, wondering how a songbird had ever learned that aerial maneuver.

She wanted to sing with joy, but remembered that female robins don't sing. Tomorrow she would seek an answer as to why that was.

HENRY HERMIT THRUSH

. . . nature's resident philosopher

It was late the next day when Robin Ray found him, a shy, solitary, hidden bird, olive-brown above with a rusty tail, and whitish below with a streaked throat and blackish-brown spots on his breast. His song was considered, by many, to be the most beautiful of any songbird. He was Uncle Henry Thrush, her relative, for she, too, was a member of the Thrush Family. He was known to all by his three names, Henry Hermit Thrush.

Although he was withdrawn to himself in the recesses of the white pines, hickories, and sumacs by his beloved pond, his loud, slow, repetitive song phrases, spiraling down the scale, resonated through the forest at dawn and at evening time.

A bright red, sunset-sky was dappling sparks of fire on the dense undergrowth at the pond's edge. As a black and white Common Loon skittered to lift from the water into the air, Robin Ray called softly, "Uncle Henry? Uncle Henry?" It was common knowledge that Henry Hermit Thrush was a bird of few words and that while impatient with the ways of mature birds, he would sometimes give short but special attention to younger ones in need of guidance.

"I heard about your mother, Robin," he said from amid the cover of a green fern thicket.

"I miss her very much Uncle Henry," she answered, moving closer. Henry Hermit Thrush did not reply; she could hear only the gentle lapping of the pond.

"Uncle Henry," she said, lowering her voice, "I have feelings . . . feelings about something I wish to do." Robin Ray's heart was beginning to beat faster.

"Good," replied the still-hidden Henry. "Intuition is the water in the pond of our consciousness. Will you follow your feelings?"

"There may be reasons not to," she added quickly, wishing he would appear.

"Caught in the branches of our own reasoning we are sometimes unable to fly. Are you afraid of what others will think, or afraid of yourself?" Uncle Henry asked, still out of view.

"Myself?" she asked, shocked. She reversed her position so that the waning sun was now at her back.

"Yes, yourself!" said Henry Hermit Thrush, forcibly, as he emerged from the ferns and stood close beside her. He cocked his head to one side and observed their shadows on the mossy ground in front of them.

"We alone cast the shadows in our own lives," said Uncle Henry. "Wherever there is darkness within us, it is because we are in the way."

In a second Robin Ray moved back to her original position and her shadow disappeared. Startled, Uncle Henry blinked.

"Do you wish to know what it is that I want, Uncle Henry?" Robin Ray asked.

"No, I do not," he replied, kindly. "I only want for you what you want for yourself. Your thought is the parent that gives birth to all things."

Henry flew to a group of smooth rocks at the edge of the pond, where pads of water lilies gently floated. Robin followed. A drop of glistening water, rosy-red from the sun's ebbing light, rolled back and forth on one of the broad lily leaves. They watched its hypnotic rocking motion for several minutes.

Henry looked out over the gentle ripples of the pond and the setting sun. "The leaf is a microcosm of the tree," he said. He pointed his head toward the lily pad. "That tiny sphere of light-reflecting water is a microcosm of the lake, and you and I are a reflection of the image of all-that-is. There is nothing in the world of nature that does not portray something in the world of spirit. You are as perfect as a snowflake."

"I shall think about that, Uncle Henry," she said quietly.

"Yes, Robin," he said, "to think about what you are thinking is an excellent beginning. All good lies on the other side of beginning again."

Beginning again? Was that possible? Robin thought of Luz and her wish that she had more lifetimes to live, that strange look in her weary eyes when she'd gazed at the clouded mountain.

As the evening light faded, Robin Ray found herself recounting her narrow escape from the falcon, her meeting with Luz, and the old Hawk's insistence upon seeing flocks of bright birds on a faraway mountain. "Could she really have seen them, Uncle Henry?" she asked.

Henry had listened carefully and now he paused before responding. "We all have a mountain to master, Robin," he said, "and whether we soar to it or valiantly struggle to climb it, all birds, all creatures, even the two-legged ones, will eventually come to know that it is what we must do. The highest mountain of all is almost always obscured by many clouds, but now and then the clouds disappear and the peak reveals itself, as if to promise, one day you will see me and know me."

Surprised at the length of his explanation, Robin Ray looked admiringly at her Uncle. She thought of his solitary life and felt sorry for him.

"Are you lonely, Uncle Henry?" she asked.

"No," he said calmly, "I am never alone. I have a constant, steadfast companion."

Robin Ray was about to ask who when Henry Hermit Thrush extended his wings, flew to the branch of a hickory tree, and began to sing the most beautiful song she had ever heard. It made her feel at peace, as though she were safe and secure under a great protective wing.

His caroling stopped abruptly.

"Robin," he said in soft twilight tones, "remember that you already know everything you need to know. Your job is to remember who you are and then tell the universe. And while you are remembering, don't forget to give thanks every day for the abundance that is already yours."

His ethereal song began again. She knew that he would not hear her goodbyes. She took flight, making a small circle over the tree where his full-hearted evensong joined the sounds of the quieting woodlands around them.

As she gained altitude to skim the darkening trees, she heard the coo of a dove and the sound of Whip-poor-wills, followed by the piercing, maniacal laugh of a loon. Then all was measureless calm.

THE CARDINALS

5

. . . a loving bond

All the birds in the garden liked the handsome pair of Northern Cardinals. If one of them seemed to be alone, a quick glimpse would always find the other nearby.

Big Red and his mate, Susie, were long-term, non-migratory residents who had never wandered far from the woods where they were born behind the gray clapboard house. They were a little shy at the hanging feeders and preferred the low shelf of sunflower seeds and cracked corn which the owner set out especially for them.

Robin Ray watched from the grape arbor as Big Red, with his scarlet crest and black face patch, carefully selected a sunflower seed. He cracked away the hard shell and tenderly placed the sweet nutmeat in Susie's red bill. She was as beautiful as he, but in a softer, more delicate way. Robin could imagine why, in times past, cardinals, the only all-red birds with crests, were caught and caged by humans.

The pair finished eating and flew to the lattice work by the potting shed. Robin admired their richness of plumage and their elegance of motion. Big Red selected a higher perch and they began a vibrant duet of song. Robin watched them playfully teasing one another, swaying back and forth in unison, and then listened in wonder as they serenaded one another with cheerful songs.

"She is singing," the young robin exclaimed. "Maybe not as loudly as he, but she *is* singing!"

Two bright red young male cardinals suddenly appeared from behind the old Oak. With an aggressive cry, Big Red took after them, leaving Susie alone.

Susie waited a moment and then took a short glide to the neatly cultivated herb garden, where she began pulling at a stalk of peppermint leaves. She stopped when she saw Robin Ray alight next to her, but was not frightened. Robins were friends with whom cardinals sometimes shared nests.

"It's still breeding season," said Susie, gently sighing.

"I don't know about breeding yet," Robin Ray responded.

"You will, my dear," Susie assured her. "I'm exhausted from nest building. I have one more to go, my third this summer, before the August molt sets in, and then I'll look ragged . . . but we love one another so it doesn't matter. Big Red especially dislikes losing his head feathers!"

Robin Ray didn't want to hear about mating and molting – she wanted to hear more about Susie's singing, and ask what she knew about the big mountain.

She started to ask about the mountain, but Susie put her off. She would think about it tomorrow, she said. Besides, was Robin Ray really sure it existed? As for singing, Susie added, Big Red had told her it was all right, so she had thought no more about it. She had sung since she was a fledgling, she said.

Wanting to get on with what she wished to do, Susie yanked loose several more peppermint leaves, sending their fragrant essence into the warm air.

"The way to health and vitality is to have an aromatic, herbal bath every day. It will soothe my tired muscles. Lavender and rosemary are very beneficial too," she added.

The lovely Cardinal picked up the fragrant leaves and flew to the birdbath. Robin Ray followed, staying on the ground below and watching. Susie dropped the leaves into the water, jumped in, and began splashing wildly, sending the scented water over the sides onto Robin Ray.

When Susie was finished, she carefully preened herself in the sunlight, fluffed her feathers, and shook her wings to dry them. Noticing that Robin Ray was watching, she turned to her and announced in a confident tone, "Enough or not, I'm all I've got. You must love your body and take good care of it. You must enjoy life each day and work with what you have today. Tomorrow may not come."

Sensing it was the proper thing to do, Robin Ray nodded in agreement.

Susie glanced in the direction of the back woods and said anxiously, "If you have anything of importance to tell me, for heaven's sake begin at the end. Otherwise I want to close my eyes and do nothing."

Robin knew she was being dismissed, so she said a quick thank you and goodbye. As she took flight to return to the top of the old Oak, she heard a sustained soft hum filtering through the leaves of the tree from the birdbath below. She had never heard it before, and it was very pleasant.

For the first time, she became aware of her own body, of the way it moved and the way it felt moving. Robin Ray liked the scent of peppermint on her wings. She would remember to have her own herbal bath soon.

THE RUDDY DUCK

6

. . . a duck for all seasons

On an especially hot summer afternoon, Robin Ray decided that she would fly to the nearby coastal marshes for some cool air.

Alighting on a stand of cattails, she spotted a brown duck with a white and black head, thick-necked and chubby-bodied, swimming in the water. She watched as he dove deep and then surfaced, cocking his spiky, partly-missing tail feathers as he swam rapidly back and forth along the surface of the water, "bubbling" it in front of him with his large cerulean blue bill.

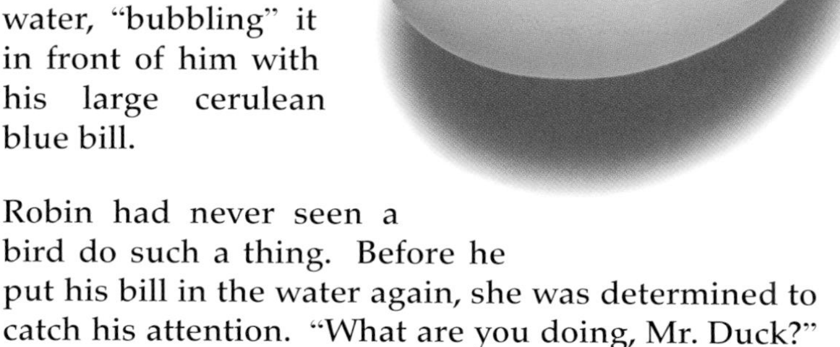

Robin had never seen a bird do such a thing. Before he put his bill in the water again, she was determined to catch his attention. "What are you doing, Mr. Duck?" she asked.

The duck paddled to the edge of the water, but did not get out. Slightly out of breath, he said, "I, Robert the Ruddy Duck, am practicing my courtship display. I'm not interested in pair bonding or looking after the young, only in mating."

"I see, Mr. Ruddy Duck," said Robin Ray. She was a little uneasy at his openness.

"You may call me Robbo – all my friends do. Are you interested in mating?" he asked forthrightly.

"Perhaps, someday," she answered shyly.

"Cool," said Robbo, "but if you have nestlings you must fledge them as quickly as possible so they can get along without you. You will be doing them a great favor in the long run."

He seemed so knowledgeable, so confident. Robin liked that.

"Also, you should take care of yourself first," Robbo said, "and in that way, you will be a better robin, not only benefiting yourself but others as well."

Robin Ray was a bit startled at that and decided to change the subject. "Have you been many places and seen many things, Robert – I mean, Robbo?" she asked. She imagined that he had.

He paddled slowly in place and said that, indeed, he had led many lives and that there were more to follow.

She listened with rapt attention as he told her about the Farallon Islands, a giant bird nursery located on the western edge of the Pacific flyway, where one half of the population of Western Gulls make their homes.

He recounted tales of more than a hundred years ago, when the islands were known as San Francisco's "egg-basket," when 600,000 murres eggs were robbed in one year for the use of the city's Great Disturbers.

Robbo emitted a loud, forceful "chuck-uk-uk" at the remembrance of that long-ago raid and started to back paddle. Robin Ray begged him to continue. He acquiesced and talked of certain species of gulls. Males are not always available to pair throughout the season so a female mates with a male and then joins another female to rear the offspring.

He told her of cuckoos and cowbirds raised by foster parents, about the bravery and the strength of particular birds he had met, such as young Bryson Gull who was raising her nestling, Maxwell, with kindness and love.

Robbo had spent a brief time in a freshwater marsh with two female Wilson's Phalaropes on their way from Canada to winter in Argentina. They told him their ways, how they were the ones who defended their territory while their mates prepared the nest and cared for the family.

In Monterey, in northern California, he had seen hundreds of Pink-footed Shearwaters, pelagic birds, who spend most of their life on the open ocean and whose parents abandon their single young before they fly.

He recalled his southern California trip, when he cruised on down to Ojai, called "the nest" by the early Indian inhabitants for the way the surrounding mountains embraced the fertile valley. How the Acorn Woodpeckers there had taught him about communal life, and how, working together, they'd stored supplies of acorns in the trunks of the oaks, sycamores, and palm trees in the valley.

"While I was in the Golden State my duck friends and I flew farther south, to the Salton Sea in the Sonoran Desert. You know it's the largest inland body of saltwater in the United States," Robbo explained almost professorially, "and a major migrating stopover on the Pacific flyway.

"The bad news," he continued, "is that in recent years it's become polluted with sewage and it has dangerous levels of salinity. Tens of thousands of birds have eaten the toxic fish, and they've been poisoned and have died. But the good news is that now a group of concerned community leaders are starting to bring this sea back to life."

"That is good news, Robbo," said Robin Ray, vigorously bobbing her head in approval.

“Seeing so many dead birds in one place was very sad,” said the Ruddy Duck. “So instead of staying there we decided to explore the cluster of Coachella Valley cities to the northwest.”

They had flown low over the even rows of date palms in Indio, he told her, and proceeded on to the desert communities of La Quinta, Indian Wells, Palm Desert, Rancho Mirage, Cathedral City, and Palm Springs. Then they'd circled back, over dozens of pristinely mowed golf courses, to one in Rancho Mirage. It had a beautiful lake, surrounded by large houses with red-tiled roofs. “Naturally, I remember the name of that wonderful place,” he boasted. “It was called Thunderbird.”

Robin Ray was listening raptly in respectful silence.

“What fun we had,” the blue-billed duck continued breezily, “relaxing in the warm sun, paddling in the cool water, and always looking up at Mount San Jacinto. It rises almost vertically from the heart of Palm Springs into the blue sky, and it was covered with snow.

“It's a true paradise, that valley,” Robbo sighed. “Maybe that's why many years ago the explorer Juan Bautista de Anza called it “La Palma de las Manos de Dios . . . The Palm of God's Hand.”

“Yes,” exclaimed Robin Ray excitedly. “I will definitely see all those things someday, Robbo!”

"Someday?" he shot back. "You do not need to listen for your creator to shout divine directions in a commanding voice, or to send an Arctic blast to catch your attention. Just do it!"

"I want to . . . I will . . . I promise," said Robin Ray. "Don't worry, I won't hide myself in a cave. I want to sing, too!"

"Good! Remember birds don't sing in caves, Robin. You will sing if you really want to."

"But Robbo, I'm a female robin," she protested weakly. "It is only the males who carol so beautifully."

"So it hasn't been done before," he said loudly. "So what! Who cares? Be the first! Start practicing and keep practicing until you learn how!

"I must fly now," said Robert the Ruddy Duck. "I'm going down to one of my favorite places, New York . . . Jamaica Bay, that is, for good food and a stay with my Green-winged and Blue-winged Teal and Canvasback duck friends. Fall is coming and we'll all be going to the Gulf Coast of Mexico for the winter."

In preparation for his ascent, he started paddling faster. Robin did not want him to go. She wanted to ask him about the shimmering birds and the cloud-covered mountain.

"When we die, do we go to a special mountain, Robbo?" she asked quickly.

"I don't know about a mountain," he answered, "but we all have a nest, a special place of refuge we can turn towards when we want to go home. Meanwhile, don't spend your time worrying about mountains or anything else that can stand in your way of making right choices in *this* life." He was paddling faster, away.

"Remember, my Robin friend . . . Robin Redbreast in a cage, would put all Heaven in a rage! Do it!"

Robin watched his long takeoff and erratic, "buzzy" bumblebee-like flight. His short wings seemed inadequate, not really up to extended migratory flight, but longer wings would get in the way of his diving for food. He appeared to be only a fun-loving bird, she thought, but Robin Ray knew that Robert the Ruddy Duck had the determination and the sheer will to make it to any destination he chose.

She watched wistfully as his handsome white rump feathers moved out of sight.

THE GREAT HORNED OWL

7

. . . wizard of the night

The light was fading and a northwestern cold front was rapidly moving in. From the flocks in the red and yellow treetops, Robin Ray could hear a wave of excitement. Southern migration would begin later this evening. As was the custom, the male robins would fly on ahead.

She could hear the distant quacking of waterfowl and other songbirds readying themselves for the journey. Robin was eager to leave, to see more, to survive until spring returned.

If she hurried, there was still time to seek counsel from the Great Horned Owl, who would not be migrating with the others. The Red-winged Blackbirds called him "a bird that makes one afraid." As she headed to the deep woods, she vowed that she would not be frightened; it was still dusk and his day would just be starting.

Deeply within the woods, she perched on a dry tree limb to listen for clues to his whereabouts. Almost immediately, a great hoot pierced the stillness, followed by a loud rasping noise like a rattlesnake. Robin Ray's feet tightly grasped the limb. The sounds seemed to be coming from far away – no, they were coming from quite near her.

Within moments, the powerful voice of an unseen owl stated, "To sharpen your sight is to increase your knowing."

Startled, she turned her head to see the Great Horned Owl silently alight at the entrance of a hollowed-out tree nest. He was very close to her. Robin Ray knew that he did not have many friends in the bird and animal kingdom – crows were his special adversaries, and he was constantly harassed by day birds who did not understand a creature different from themselves.

As he positioned himself to stare at her, with his cat-like face and wide-set ear tufts, she noticed his feather-taloned feet. They helped silence his approach and could also seize and kill. She looked at his rapier bill, which could tear flesh into pieces for his nestlings and his personal consumption. She would be careful in her questioning and remain alert at all times, she decided.

"You must sharpen your sight," he said authoritatively, blinking his eyes to emphasize the importance of his words. "I trust that you have come here to learn."

Robin nodded and started to speak, only to be quickly cut off by the giant Owl.

"My nights are taken up in study and research, my days ruminating on all that I have learned. The less you speak, the more you hear!" he said, eyeing her carefully. "What is your subject of interest?"

In one long breath, with her eyes closed and with a rapid-fire delivery, she asked, "Why don't female robins sing? I want to – to sing!"

"Sing?" he asked incredulously. "A female robin songster?

"You are a vain bird," he said, "if you do not see that harmony consists in truth alone, which is for a few special birds only and gained by laborious study, not by engaging yourself with singing."

"But," Robin protested, "I feel that I could sing."

"Could? Feel? What have feelings got to do with it? Female robins do *not* sing!" he screeched.

The Great Horned Owl flexed his feathered talons, quivered with half-suppressed rage, and raised his wings in a vast circle about his body. His eyes flashing fiercely, he continued.

"Ignorance is the curse, knowledge the wind whereby we fly to heaven! There is necessity for hard choices, constant discipline, for obedience, for lessons to be learned, for carrying forth the legacy of our ancestors!" he pontificated vigorously.

Robin Ray did not want to become fearful, having learned from Uncle Henry that fear attracts like energy and that it could be dangerous in her current situation.

"Yes," she quickly agreed, wondering if he would attack her in his fury. "Ignorance is a curse. It is neglectful to remain without wisdom." But ignorant of what, ignorant of whom?

He barely acknowledged her statement, but it seemed to soothe him. He continued his monologue. "There are laws of nature – an order to the world, ceaseless rhythms, seasons, ebb and flow, times and tides, courting, nesting, hatching, fledging, molting, migratory cycles that are irreversible, inevitable. To live and endure you must fully understand this. When you do, you will be wise."

Darkness was setting in. She would ask no more about singing. Besides, she thought, a stuffy old bird like him would never understand! And surely any questions about the mountain would have to wait. Obviously he would consider her very stupid to have to ask about a smooth-domed mountain she was not absolutely certain she had seen.

Even if this supposedly very wise bird did have an explanation, thought Robin Ray, he probably would withhold the answer from her in order to enhance his own position and power.

The owl fixed his eyes on her intently. They were now narrowed to slits, she saw. "Any bird can see in full daylight," he said. "But when nightfall comes, only those with the sharpest vision can survive in the dark forest."

Then he was off, silently gliding, an apparition, drifting in and out of sight between the dark trees. Then he was gone, leaving only his resonant hoot and Robin Ray's unanswered questions hanging in the night air.

SOUTHERN MIGRATION

. . . an ancestral ritual

For the last twenty-five million years, the ritual of fall migration had moved many, many billions of neo-tropical migrant birds – those birds that nest north of the Tropic of Cancer – to their wintering grounds in the New World tropics.

From mid-September to early November, depending on the severity of the weather, more than 340 species of birds complete their molting, store additional body fat, and then take to the air for their long southern journeys.

For Robin Ray and her fellow flock, it would start as a nocturnal flight moving south along the eastern seaboard. They would cross the Gulf, bypassing the Caribbean, and then funnel down the throat of Mexico to the narrow corridor of Central America.

Flying in flocks of three to three hundred at mile-high altitudes, with an average of twenty in each group, they would endure the twice-a-year risks of migration to secure optimum nesting in the north and find available food, especially insects, in the warmer habitats in the south.

Winter for them would mean relaxation from reproductive responsibilities, and a scarcity of birds for the domestic and feral cats in the north, who kill two to three million birds a day. During this time, another 100 million to 1 billion of them would be saved from collisions with man-made structures, including the reflective glass that mimics the sky.

Observing that the stars around the North Pole rotated the least, and using that fixed, unmoving North Star as a compass, Robin Ray followed the others as they exploited the winds and compensated for wind drift, flying with great precision at the optimal altitude, usually below 2000 feet, for minimizing energy expenditure and maximizing speed.

Keeping a steady pace of between fifteen and twenty-five miles an hour, they would cover 250 miles in one night, making stopovers for food and rest, sometimes for a single day or sometimes for as long as a week.

During the day while the flock rested they were safe from broad-winged hawks and other raptors who soared, using thermal updrafts and the position of the sun to guide them to their southern destinations.

Despite what Robin Ray had been told about the perils of night migration, she was happy to be back in the dark sky, hearing the sharp and often melodious peeping calls from the other birds keeping in touch with one another. They warned of deadly hazards such as aircraft, or being dashed blindly against the high television towers that cause the greatest mortality among birds. Another danger was a quick down-draft of air that could hurl them against mountainsides or drown them in the rivers or lakes below.

Most feared by all of the night flyers was a sudden change in weather. If a leading edge called a cold front – an area of high pressure – meets with warmer air, then clouds, rain, lightning, hail, snow and ice could form. Robin Ray knew that if any of these elements rapidly closed in on her flock, it would mean disaster. As if to outfly that thought, she moved her wings faster.

During the nights that followed, Robin Ray learned more about the dangers and wonders of migration. Although she was burning her body fat quickly, the fifty percent more sugar in her warm blood than humans would keep her temperature at one-hundred-and-ten degrees Fahrenheit, the highest of all animals.

One of her migration teachers, an older female robin with one missing toe, called by the flock "Three Toes," told her that geese and other birds who fly in V formations use far less energy pushing aside the air than do songbirds who fly singly. "Geese in the Himalayas migrate at heights of more than thirty-one thousand feet, and condors in the Andes fly at more than nineteen thousand feet," said Three Toes matter-of-factly. It feels good to know, thought Robin Ray.

Sensing her growing interest in learning, the older robin described in detail ducks who can travel up to a thousand miles in a single day. Hearing this, Robin

Ray peeped loudly, momentarily disrupting the rhythmic flapping of the birds around her.

She calmed herself by thinking of the others. Suppose I were an Arctic Tern, the bird who travels farthest, every year making a twenty-two-thousand-mile round trip to the Antarctic? Or the tiniest migrant, a Ruby-throated Hummingbird? Her mother had told her that they weigh only four-and-a-half grams, less than the smallest acorn, half of which is body fat energy. She knew that in crossing the Gulf, Ruby-throats sometimes fly 500-600 miles in about 16-18 hours. No – she would not complain; she would just keep moving.

"Chimney Swifts, with long narrow wings and short weak legs, probably never alight on the ground," said her instructor emphatically, "as it's doubtful they could ever take off. These nearly full-time aerialists capture insects, drink, bathe, and even court while they're flying. And some swifts fly non-stop for up to three years and rest only to breed." Three Toes swerved abruptly off to the right to reprimand two young robins who were flying too close together for safety.

Robin Ray was left mentally exhausted by this last morsel of information. I'm certainly glad that I'm not a Chimney Swift, she thought.

The flock swept on. At last, sensing from the sweet smell of the tropical night air that her migration journey was almost over, Robin Ray gazed at the seven-starred Constellation of the Great Bear. "It's very beautiful up here," she said softly, "but now it's time to see our winter home."

It was the break of a new day late in October when Robin Ray's acute color vision picked up the first signs of a Central American emerald valley sliding toward the sea.

Having observed, analyzed, and synthesized all the ancestral cues available in nature, the polarized light, radiation, barometric pressure, subtle olfactory cues, and variations in the earth's magnetic field, she had arrived! For the first time, she was seeing a panoramic view of the landmarks long familiar to her ancestral songbird family.

As was the custom, the male migrants had already laid claim to the mature habitat. She and the other females settled into their less-than-pristine territory. The flight had seasoned her and she welcomed the coming of the light.

THE RESPLENDENT QUETZAL

. . . friend of the earth

How much I have seen, how much I have learned here these past months, Robin Ray thought as she watched the cumulus clouds expanding over the mountains.

She was listening to a flock of older resident birds. They were mournfully telling how the dangers of loss of habitat, pesticides, the removal of native flowering plants, even the slingshots used by the human natives of the area, were taking a dramatic toll on migration. Two-thirds of the neo-tropical migrants were now uncommon, rare, or locally extinct.

Robin Ray had seen for herself some of the monocultures of cattle, sugar, and bananas that had replaced significant amounts of Mexico and Central America's rainforest ecosystems with fields that were useless to wildlife.

"More than ninety-nine percent of the species that have been alive are not with us today, gone," said an alarmed Blue-crowned Motmot, speaking with a rhythmical, low-pitched, hooting sound. Sitting on a prominent perch, his graduated racquet-tipped tail swung from side to side, like a pendulum that had lost much of its momentum.

Other birds chimed in with their own knowledge, and the sad stories continued until Robin Ray could hear no more.

With a fast-beating heart, she lifted her wings and fled to the dark canopy of the montane evergreen forest that was situated on the windward slope of the mountains. She settled in a high tree just as some fat tropical raindrops, *pelo de gato*, started to fall onto the forest floor from the ends of the tank bromeliads, the miniature orchids, and the overarching Inga trees.

She would wait for the rain to stop before she returned to the others, she decided, take in the exotic beauty and incredible diversity of the rainforest plant and animal life. The stillness of the forest and the soft rain falling from the pointed "drip-tips" of the leaves were comforting. Robin Ray closed her eyes, mourning quietly for its dim future.

Suddenly, a noisy fast-flying group of multi-colored tanagers and orioles raced by, zooming in and out of the lower branches. Robin Ray turned to see them and in that instant, carefully concealed on the limb above her, a large tropical snake struck with a powerful blow to her head, knocking her to the wet forest floor. Her wings disheveled, she lay there unconscious.

The snake was rapidly slithering down the tree to finish off its prey when from under the top of the high, lush canopy a bird swooped down. Streamlining its long, glittering-green tail feathers and its rainbowed wings and body, it swiftly descended with a loud, threatening "caw!" The frightened reptile dropped to the ground and quickly disappeared into a hole at the base of the well-rooted tree.

Now the multi-hued bird approached Robin Ray and watched closely as her eyes slowly opened. She looked up at him through blurred eyes that went in and out of focus, shifting between his forest-green head and the pink and red young leaves at the top of the high canopy a hundred feet above them.

"You are a lucky bird," the Resplendent Quetzal said gently.

After several attempts at focusing her eyes, Robin could now clearly see the bird she had heard so much about. Standing before her was a creature so elegant and green that he looked as if he were painted with crushed emeralds. Tinged with pure molten gold, his feathered front was as red as the blood of a thousand Mayan sacrifices. He was the most beautiful bird she had ever seen!

She hopped up, still dizzy.

"It is a different kind of jungle here, my Robin friend!" he warned her. "Next time, you might not be so lucky. You northern birds must remember that the rules of nature apply here too, in full force!"

Still shaken, Robin smoothed her wing feathers, grateful to be alive.

"You must go back to your friends now," the Resplendent Quetzal said. "It is getting late. This is no place for a robin after dark. What brought you here?"

Robin Ray told him what she had heard about the destruction of the rainforest and the decreasing migration. "Is it true?" she asked gravely.

"If you are truly concerned, come back tomorrow," he told her. "Bring others and join our Council of Birds, who want to save our earth, our home. My name is Guy," he said, flying up to a high tree branch. "I love this earth! We must protect it. I'm hoping that I'll see you tomorrow Robin."

From then on, Robin Ray returned each afternoon, day after day, bringing with her more and more other birds to hear Guy's wisdom and warnings. Never seeming to tire of his subject, he would move back and forth along his perching limb, his long tail feathers moving in rhythm with his steps, his voice modulating from low, intimate sounds to strident cries.

One day he began by saying, "Whether it has eyes or not, every creature has some way of seeing its world –

some way of getting information about its environment. All species must work out their mutual experiences, their consistency with one another.

"Our earth is four-and-a-half billion years old," he said. If we could squeeze those billions of years into twenty-four hours, we can appreciate that humans have only been around for the last minute. And only in the last few seconds have people formed settled societies. If they manage to stay around in their present form, as long as we birds have, or as long as whales have, they have many millions of years to go."

"They still are very immature!" buzzed Josephina, a tiny, darting Green-throated Mountain-gem hummingbird. She stopped and hovered close to Guy, whirring in place.

"You are right," Guy said. "They need to learn more about taking responsibility. Humans have managed to survive four Ice Ages, but they are a threat to our planet as well as a promise. In just a few hundred years, a blink of an eye by the earth's standards, the brash young human species has destroyed vast, natural ecosystems and transformed our environment. No animal piles up food or takes land beyond its need as they do."

A brightly colored large-billed old Toucan appeared from a nest hole in the tree gallery. He ruffled his plumage and said harshly, "Humankind will inevitably meet with disaster, for their survival, as well as ours, is subject to nature's laws!"

There was a raucous ripple of consent, of shrill caws and cries, to the old Toucan's words.

"Perhaps," said Guy. "But humans are an experiment in freedom, and a risky one. When they gained freedom of choice, called free will, and a subconscious that accepts and stores everything thought or spoken, they also gained consciousness – an awareness of what they are doing – and the capacity to remember what they have done. The problem seems to be that they have used their consciousness to predict only the immediate consequences of their behavior, but they have failed to consider the broader, long-range result of their choices."

"If only they could fly up as high as we do and see how they have befouled their own nests," said an irate Barred Woodcreeper, perched halfway up a bromeliad-covered tree trunk.

Two Dot-winged Antwrens looked up from the forest floor but added nothing to the discussion and went back to studying a marching ant army.

"There is, however, some hope," Guy said. And Robin Ray thought she had heard somewhere before about hope perching in the soul and just singing and singing. She liked the word "hope."

She thought of the tree-shaded coffee plantations she had seen being planted just a valley away. Instead of clearing fully exposed "sun hedge" plantations that were unfriendly to wildlife, humans once again had begun to grow their crops in the shade to provide a favorable habitat for the birds. It was a small step in the right direction, Robin thought. But was there time for them to learn more?

"There has been some promising progress," Guy was saying, "but there remains a great deal for them to do to clean the air, clean the water, and dispose of their waste materials in a fashion that sustains the earth instead of spoiling it. If they could do this, it could usher in a new millennium of integrity, sweetness, and light," he said thoughtfully.

With sharp, rattling high-notes, the doubting Toucan shouted, "Sweetness, ha! What a ridiculous word! They don't deserve to survive!"

Unperturbed, Guy continued. "Although they seek and search everywhere outside themselves for answers – in meetings, books, lectures, leaders, and personalities – I do not believe that failure is written on the human horizon. It is, rather, a deep homesickness, which I think can never be satisfied with anything less than a clear awareness of the higher power they possess."

The birds were quiet, listening to his words.

"If they use their human ability to write and communicate," Guy said, "to store information and pass it on to future generations – if they think about and question ideas rather than just let a few powerful individuals dictate to them – they may be able to act before it is too late, to restore balance, order, and harmony with nature."

Guy was ending his urgent discussion on a somewhat optimistic note, but Robin Ray still felt saddened by what she had learned.

It was late March and she was beginning to miss her northern home. She missed the sight of the human being who always filled the birdbath and provided food for her and her friends. Guy had told the assembly that in the United States there were more than eighty million people like her, called bird watchers.

"I know we have harmony with those human beings," she said half-aloud. "But I am very worried about the others."

RETURNING NORTH

. . . riding the winds together

10

In the shaded coffee plantation where she loved to go alone, Robin Ray met her mate, a handsome, large Robin with sensitive eyes.

She was just finishing a complicated song pattern when he gave a call to attract her attention. "How unusual it is to hear a female robin sing so beautifully," he said. "Where did you learn to do that?"

Robin was startled, and very pleased at his open acceptance of her singing. She looked at him carefully and felt certain she had seen him at one of Guy's meetings.

"I'm glad you like my song," she said. "I taught myself to sing during the spring migration. And I convinced some other female migrants to start practicing too."

The large Robin was looking at her warmly, she thought.

"At first it was difficult," she continued, "because I was trying to duplicate the male robin's notes and phrasing, but after a while I became uncomfortable with that and decided to practice the songs in my own way, so that the meaning could be understood by all, but it was still my voice being heard."

"How did the male robins respond to your singing?" he asked.

Robin Ray hesitated briefly and then said, "Just fine," not telling him that it was still only when she was well hidden in the trees that she would sing out.

"Do you think Guy is right about there being hope for our future?" she asked, attempting to change the subject.

He moved closer to her and said, with a kind, strong voice, "We are always quick to notice depletion rather than munificence. But I would agree with Guy that even though the problems are very great, they can be solved."

Before the afternoon was over, Robin Ray had fallen in love with this optimistic Robin. Within the next few days they decided to abandon the usual tradition of the males flying on ahead and to fly north together, to start a family in the same nesting Oak behind the gray clapboard house where she had been born.

It was the beginning of the yearly bird migration north. They would leave early before the air was crowded with songbirds returning home. Using an ancient, three-pillared temple ruin as their primary landmark, and under the light of a full moon, they mounted high into the sky to ride the winds together. The constant North Star would guide them safely home, they hoped.

THE MOURNING DOVE

. . . ray of light

The long journey northward was finally completed. As they had planned, Robin Ray's mate laid immediate territorial claim to the old Oak and the familiar garden. The last traces of snow from an early spring storm had disappeared and the robins were eager to begin their family.

But day by day, as they began gathering small twigs, grasses, and other nesting materials, Robin Ray became alarmed. Many changes had taken place in the garden during her absence.

The old Oak and the trees in the back woods had leafed out, and the scarlet firethorn bushes and forsythia were in bud. But the neatly cultivated rows of annuals that always flourished in the brick-lined flower beds had not been planted. Weeds had completely taken over the perennial flower plots where peony, hollyhock, foxglove, and daisy had bloomed. And the birdbath remained dry.

Soon Robin Ray noticed that the hanging feeders had been removed and were lying with a messy pile of debris near the back porch of the house. A rusted metal FOR SALE sign protruded from the pile, half-obscured by a broken children's bicycle. Robin Ray wondered where the kind homeowner was.

Then all became clear. A new family of four now inhabited the gray clapboard house, but no one among them was nature- or bird-friendly. For the family's two noisy sons, sport consisted of practice with bb guns. They used a bulls-eye attached to the lattice on the side of the potting shed, or threw cans into the air as targets for the wooden slingshots they often carried.

Dawn was breaking and Robin Ray's concerns faded with the stars into the early light. Her thoughts had been interrupted by the sound of cows lowing from the nearby farm and by the call of a Mourning Dove, repeating itself in the air of the dawn. Her nest was now completed, and as the cloudless sky deepened to a richer blue, Robin headed in the direction of the farm.

She heard the dove's call again as she approached the open-doored red barn. It stood under a mighty Ash tree with massive, branching arms and serrated leaves that had the appearance of small green flames.

Several hungry geese and chickens were scrambling after the morning's pickings; a small flock of sheep and two oxen stood by, unconcerned about the feeding ritual.

Robin heard the dove's call again, the low, sweet *coo-AH-cooo-cooo-coo* now at close range. She glided down from the Ash tree to the entrance of the barn and saw, in the suffused light, on a bale of hay, a fawn-colored Mourning Dove, placing one foot in front of the other, moving back and forth, jerking its head with each stride, as if to emphasize its words.

Under the Dove's tutelage, two young dove squabs pecked at a mound of seeds on the barn floor, carefully discarding certain ones to the side. "Thoughts are like seeds, and when held in mind produce their own kind," the Mourning Dove was telling the young ones. "You must choose your seeds wisely."

She looked up and saw Robin watching intently. The mother dove welcomed her in. "These are my children, Jonah and Joy," she said, "and I am their mother, Jessie. I'm teaching my two about seed thoughts, and that we birds are the link between earthbound creatures and the distant wonders of the heavens and the power that controls them."

"Who . . . what is that power?" Robin asked.

"It has always been a mystery," Jessie replied, "but I believe we are all part of the higher power. Just as the sun, earth, moon, and sea are common to us all, though they are called different names among the different birds, so our creator, who orders all things, has different honors and titles given according to the laws of the flocks."

"How does our creator make his presence known?" asked Robin.

"Our creator, or as some of the human ones call Him . . . or Her, God, Yahweh, Allah, Krishna, Father, Mother, the Great Spirit, will get the message through to you – how to listen, how to understand, how to find your way. But you will come to that understanding along the path of your heart, not the journey of your mind," Jessie said knowingly.

"I still have much to learn," Robin said. She and Jessie watched Jonah and Joy follow a pair of yellow-winged butterflies out the barn door.

"It doesn't matter how the understanding and knowledge is gained," Jessie replied. "Great teachers such as Jesus, Buddha, Moses, Muhammad, lived to enlighten many of our earth's creatures. Since we have many lifetimes to choose and re-choose our soul paths, we must listen to the still voice deep within us and unfold our own lives as we see fit."

"But suppose Jonah and Joy, or I, Robin Ray, choose things that harm us without knowing it?" she questioned.

"From time to time you will," Jessie assured her, "but all experience is part of learning. You need only remember what you are trying to master, which is yourself."

Jessie moved her eyes in a sweeping motion around the barn. "We will eventually come to realize that all this is really insubstantial. The only true substance in the universe is this invisible force, this higher power.

You may use it by the simple acceptance of knowing that it exists, and then letting it come forth at your command."

"At my command?" Robin Ray was perplexed. "It is you who seems so knowing . . . so powerful!" A gentle breeze entered the barn, and the hanging milk pails on the lowest rafter swayed very gently back and forth.

"Boldness is called for!" said Jessie. "We must quit hoping and wishing and set about doing and being."

Robin Ray nodded. "I am strong. I shall grow in understanding."

"Yes, you will, Robin, and by constantly blessing and giving thanks to this higher power you will increase its flow." Still pacing back and forth on the bale of hay, Jessie said, "Guard your own life from all ignorant intrusion. Protect yourself from any thought or act which would involve you in anything but the fuller and more harmonious expression of life."

Jessie moved behind the bale of hay. Robin Ray heard a quick scratching among the straws and she reappeared, holding a smooth, red berry in her bill. She placed it gently at Robin Ray's feet. "This special berry that I give to you, Robin, is the color of love and the heart's blood – both necessary for a good life."

Robin looked at the berry closely.

“Please take it as a symbol of the greatest gift bestowed on us by our creator,” said Jessie, “that of unconditional love for us.”

“I am grateful, Jessie. I shall keep it always,” Robin Ray promised.

“Many great souls have lived and their works have passed with them, because they were unconscious of the power that sustained them. Had they recognized this power, their accomplishments would have stood forth as a mountain.”

Robin Ray was about to ask Jessie about the faraway mountain when Jessie took a quick step forward. “Come, close now, and listen, my dear Robin.”

Robin obeyed quickly.

Jessie lowered her voice. “Our creator teaches us that love is all there is . . . however, for us to know and understand love fully, the infinite one asks that . . . ”

The rest was whispered to Robin Ray as Jonah and Joy flew into the barn and up to the rafters, chased by two loudly quacking geese, who, seeing they could not catch them, quickly departed.

“Why do they chase us, Mother?” asked Jonah.

“Come down, little ones,” Jessie said quietly. “It is time to talk about conditions in life that can never be resolved by running away.”

Saying good-bye would not be easy, but Robin knew it was time to return to her nest, to start laying her eggs. She picked up the red berry in her bill and moved toward the barn door. As she took flight, she heard Jessie say, "Take no thought for tomorrow, Robin, for tomorrow shall take care of itself. There is only this moment . . . NOW!"

The rest of the day passed quickly. Robin laid her first glossy blue egg right next to Jessie's red berry, which she had carefully placed in the bottom of her nest. She felt a sense of deep contentment, and her only concern was the absence of the one who no longer fed the birds.

Just before she fell asleep, Robin Ray heard the soft cooing of a Mourning Dove. She would never hear a dove's call again without remembering Jessie's secret whispered words. The meaning of its call, *coo-AH-cooo-cooo-coo,* was LOVE ME . . . WE ARE ONE! Robin Ray wondered how it was that Jessie had come to know that meaning. She said it over and over again, LOVE ME . . . WE ARE ONE, until she fell peacefully asleep.

FLYING UPWARD

12

. . . an immutable continuity

Robin Ray had now laid four eggs, and she and her loving mate joyfully anticipated their new family. Tomorrow would be the day they had waited for.

At first light, Robin was awakened by a cock's crowing, followed by the noise of a loudly banging door. She stood up in the nest and watched as the man from the house below emerged from the back porch carrying two suitcases. He loaded them into the trunk of the red sedan in the driveway.

As the man carried a second load of baggage to the car, his two sons kicked open the back door and ran toward the center of the lawn between the house and the old Oak tree. The younger boy was holding a long, coiled rope with a rectangular slab of wood attached to the end of it. He uncoiled it and began to whirl it rapidly around his head, faster and faster until it emitted a fluttering roar.

As the whizzing sound became more furious, his older brother took the slingshot from his belt. Yelling with glee, he picked up a small, round rock from near the birdbath, placed it in the strong rubber bands of the slingshot, and pulled back hard as he aimed. The stone shot forth and missed the circling wooden target by only a few inches. At tremendous speed, it hurtled into the upper branches of the old Oak, just as the boys' mother noisily shut the door of the back porch.

"Stop it right now, the two of you . . . get in the car!" she called. She locked the door and walked quickly toward her waiting husband, now seated behind the wheel of the car, whose motor was already running. She and the boys got in and slammed the doors, and the car moved down the gravel driveway with a loud crunching sound.

In the old Oak tree, when the deadly stone projectile hit Robin Ray's black and white striped throat, she felt nothing; she was only aware of total darkness, and wings so heavy that she could not move them.

What seemed like an eternity later, Robin Ray's wings were still leaden. Out of the black sky, the end of a silver string appeared at the tip of her bill; she felt a strange familiarity and opened her mouth to take hold of it. With a gentle up-shaft of air, Robin Ray was guided over the old Oak tree, the familiar garden, the potting shed, past the back woods, and towards the nearby farm with the red barn and the mighty Ash tree.

The Ash tree's leaves were now alive with crackling flames, leaping high into the air. With the silver string still grasped tightly in her bill, she was moved directly above the center of the fierce glow.

As fiery tendrils reached out for her, she tried to fly upward, but her wings would not move, her bill would not open. She hung suspended and helpless, looking down in panic, watching the seething flames begin a rapid rotary motion that formed a spiraling, raging column of fire. She was being drawn into an ever-widening whirlpool, a fierce and grinding vortex that seemed ready to engulf her.

"I don't want to die!" Robin Ray screamed out in terror. "Up . . . Up . . . NOW!" she begged, losing hold of the string.

In seconds she recovered it, and with all of her might, pulled on the silver lifeline. There was no response.

Then with a roaring, deafening sound, the still-burning mighty Ash tree was violently uprooted, its leaves ripped and flying like a million giant fireflies as it was consumed in the vortex. Robin Ray could feel the silver string loosening and knew that she was being pulled under too. Her last thoughts would be, "I don't want to die! I want to live!"

Seconds later, the string became taut and she was lifted upward, over a stand of tall evergreens. The mighty Ash tree disappeared into the flames, and with one final malevolent roar, the pit of fire closed over in the dark night.

As she rose higher into the sky, Robin Ray's wings now moved with pure delight. She noticed that her pale red breast feathers had turned a bright brick red. She had made her escape . . . she was moving through space and time, careless of the eighteen-billion-year-old world below, about to become part of an immutable continuity.

Robin Ray had no idea how long she had floated free. With the string still clenched in her yellow bill, she looked below and saw flowing-tailed comets of vibrant color spiraling upward toward her from a glimmering, blue-marble planet Earth. They were moving her into a warm, prismatic thermal of birds of every color, of every hue, tint, and tinge.

With a surge of joy, she saw she was one of them, birds from all continents, all countries, all habitats, polar, grasslands, tropical forests, deserts, mountains, islands, rivers and lakes, coast and oceans, all flying upward in perfect harmony.

THE NEST

13

. . . a special place

From out of a blinding cloud of colored light, a glowing male American Robin flew toward her on noiseless wings, took the silver string in his bill, and guided her upward to the edge of a gigantic nest woven of millions of similar strings. Robin Ray knew at once that this robin was her father. She opened her mouth to speak, but no words came out.

Then, at breathtaking speed, her father propelled them both in a circle around the nest, weaving her string tightly into it. Robin Ray was struck with awe at the immense size of the nest.

As they completed the circle, Robin Ray realized that seven birds were stationed equidistant around the rim, facing outward as guardians of what lay within it. A Sharp-shinned Hawk, a Hermit Thrush, a Cardinal, a Ruddy Duck, a Great Horned Owl, a Resplendent Quetzal, and a Mourning Dove. Her father silently guided her to the side of the Sharp-shinned Hawk, and vanished into the light.

She was startled to recognize a youthful Luz, who immediately indicated that they would be communicating with each other through the inaudible sounds called high vibrations, the way that was used in this realm of understanding.

"Yes Robin, I have learned that we do have many lifetimes. I am young again . . . and yes, that was your father, who is beginning to understand that all who fly without light are birds that have strayed from the nest. The nest is always here to return to."

So Robert the Ruddy Duck was right, thought Robin. We all have a nest, a special place of refuge. She was observing that she could understand Luz's thoughts completely.

"My mother, Luz, is she here too? Is she all right?" asked Robin wordlessly, trying out her new skill and deciding not to ask more about her father.

"Yes, she is. Your mother was with us for only a short while, Robin," Luz replied, "but you will meet her again, someday . . . in another time, in another place."

"I will, Luz?" Robin Ray was relieved. "And what about the seven guardians of the nest? I know them from the past, don't I?"

"Yes," responded Luz, "they are symbols of those who came into your life, to teach you something you needed to know. As one flies up to the mountain, the kinds of birds that come into our lives are different for everyone. Your time on earth was an opportunity to discover much of this knowledge."

"Have I reached the mountain, Luz?" asked Robin expectantly.

"You have," the young Hawk responded, her eyes alive. "This is the top of the mountain that bears you above the earthly fog line of doubt, fear, sickness, disappointment, and failure. Here ·you are healed, life is renewed."

"So you did see a faraway mountain, Luz?" Robin asked. "And are there flocks of shimmering birds, too?"

"Yes Robin. Birds just like you, who have come to be nurtured by a power that has been indestructible down through the ages. One that was fully established long before the advent of all the creatures of the earth."

Robin Ray's attention was taken by a stream of slow-moving light that arose from the nest and moved out of sight.

Luz continued knowingly. "If you nurture this power with love, reverence, and devotion, it becomes a habit and soon it becomes part of your existence. You will start slowly . . . and as you are faithful over a few things, and perfect them, you will become master over all things."

"And how do I nurture this power?" Robin asked.

"By becoming one with it. But to do this you must persevere and keep practicing, because you are still on the treadmill of not knowing."

“Not knowing, Luz?”

“Yes, not knowing what spirit is,” Luz explained. “Spirit is everywhere . . . forever! But we cannot put a single definition on it.”

“Then was spirit in the vortex?” asked Robin, not quite sure that she fully understood.

“Yes,” Luz said, “even there. The lesson to be learned from the vortex is that not expressing that which spirit has conceived for you is very similar to experiencing the searing vortex of a life not fully lived.

“Robin,” she continued, “Spirit is ever-present – in the vortex, in the blossom . . . even in the scent of the flower. In all humanity. All things.”

Robin thought of the afternoon with Uncle Henry – the tiny droplet of water on the lily pad, and his words about nature reflecting the world of spirit.

Luz gently guided Robin closer to the inner edge of the nest. She patiently explained that the nest is very much like one’s own consciousness, woven together to hold something precious, something to nurture and protect.

“Do you remember the smooth dome of the mountain that you thought you saw, Robin, on the day you believed that I had died?”

Robin nodded her head, remembering the swirling clouds and the fleeting scene with the rainbow.

"Now you will come to know where this supreme power resides eternally, and how you are already part of it, Robin."

They had arrived at the edge of the nest. They were standing close together, and Robin Ray could now see that embraced within it, bathed in a soft aura of radiant pink light, was spirit egg.

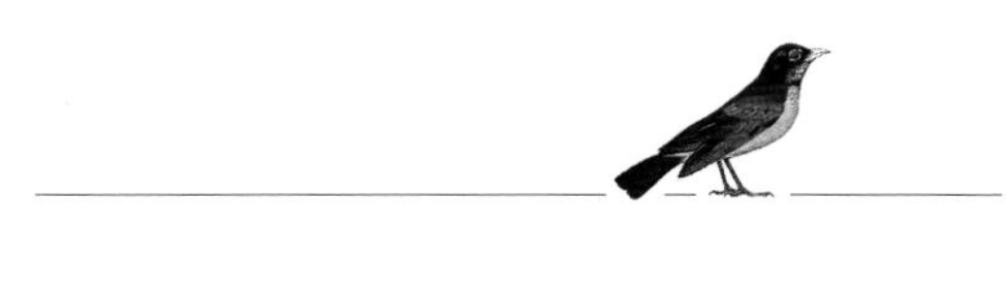

SPIRIT EGG

. . . birds of a feather

14

Emanating from within the huge, translucent spirit egg, precisely centered in the carefully woven nest, she saw great flocks of birds of different colors, some beginning to glow and shimmer in the light. All shapes and sizes were nestled closely together on this perfectly formed, rosy, speckled, smooth-shelled egg. Robin watched as every minute, hundreds of new birds kept filling the nest. How had an egg of such incredible beauty been created?

"So this is spirit egg!" she murmured, watching in wonder as one bird after another chose its place and settled down on the surface. "Will they nurture it until it comes forth?" she asked Luz.

"Yes, they will," the young Hawk replied, "but it will take the warmth of all the birds and the leaders of their flocks to do it."

Robin had a million questions, and wanted to tell Luz about Guy and what she remembered about the importance of working together to find solutions.

As if reading her thoughts, Luz said, "There is much more for you to remember, Robin. You must now communicate directly with spirit egg." Luz moved close behind her and Robin felt a quiver of excitement and fear.

"Don't be afraid, Robin," said Luz, instructing her, "the actual starting point is right within your own body.

"By absorbing the love and the beauty of spirit egg, you allow the light essence to come in. Then you will be able to generate and transform this energy so that it can be sent out from you to others. You may begin whenever you are ready, Robin."

If Uncle Henry was right, thought Robin, that all good lies on the other side of beginning again, then I am ready to begin. With an effortless glide, she joined the others, easing her body down to make contact with the pulsating pink egg.

The heat radiating from the warm egg and from the two birds on either side of her, an Evening Grosbeak and an Anna's Hummingbird, and the rhythmic beat from within the egg, made her drowsy. Tucking her head under her slate-gray wing, which was now beginning to glow slightly, she fell sound asleep.

Her head was still under her wing when her eyes were swiftly drawn to a beam of pure white light piercing through the rosy, opaque substance within spirit egg and leading into the exact center of it. At the end of the laser-like beam, Robin became aware of slow, intermittent bursts of light. They were illuminating some words that floated, in an undulating motion, on the rosy surface.

As the steady beat continued, she watched the words appear, linger, for a moment, blend into the next one, and then disappear. They began . . . COURAGE . . . HARMONY . . . JOY . . . PEACE . . . and continued, one by one, until Robin could feel a new level of energy pouring through her body, a new awareness of the meaning of each word.

She knew she was ready to learn more. The steady beat and the rocking motion from spirit egg continued. More words appeared.

Come to me, now, just as you are!

We never die, just change form. Life can never be destroyed.

She remembered the old Hawk, Luz, and her wish that there were many lifetimes to live, and her own fear and terror that she would die in the vortex.

Remember only the things that you wish to retain.

Be humble. Heal your troubled heart.

She remembered her mother's devotion, the kindness of the old woman who loved birds . . . and all the others who had befriended her.

Forget what you do not want to remember.

By forgiving yourself first, you can forgive others.

She would forget those who had tried to harm her, especially her father, whom she could now completely forgive for the pain he had caused.

Have no fear nor false pride, ask for guidance.

Your most dangerous enemy is yourself.

She remembered Uncle Henry, and now she knew who his constant companion was. She thought of his lesson of her shadow on the mossy ground, and her standing in her own way.

Do what you feel is right, it is deeds that endure.

Your own work counts, not what somebody else has done.

She remembered the wisdom of the Great Horned Owl, and now she understood the importance of self-discipline and knowledge. But she was still glad she had followed her own feelings about singing, doing what was right for her.

Give of yourself with the purest of intention.

The will to serve keeps life flowing.

She remembered the teachings of Guy, the benevolent Resplendent Quetzal, his concern for the environment, and his reverence and true compassion for all the creatures of the earth.

Your choices create the universe you see.

An honorable life harmonizes with your inner nature.

She remembered the spontaneous, free, and happy Robert the Ruddy Duck, and the choices he had made to be true to himself, to see more of the world – to be open-minded to others and tolerant of the lives they lived.

In perfect love all things are united.

Believe and receive, with gratitude and love.

She remembered the loving bond between the pair of Cardinals . . . their ability to have fun and enjoy each day together . . . and the loyalty and love of her own mate . . . and how, with all her heart she'd had faith that she would sing, and did!

Be true to your vision, from your vision comes the seed.

Spirit is the primary, originating power.

She remembered Jessie, the Mourning Dove, her words about the importance of "seed thoughts," and her gift of the red berry, the color of love.

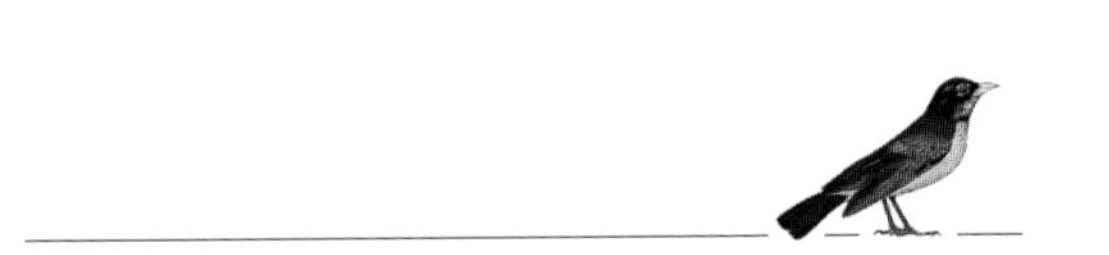

THE JOURNEY

. . . a sacred communion

Robin did not know how long the healing, rocking motion continued. A feeling of contentment and peace, a feeling she had never known before, enveloped her.

Robin Ray now understood that all that came from spirit egg must return to it. To be complete, the creatures of the universe must join closely together to nurture spirit egg, listen to its wisdom, and then stand as guardians of the nest until the beauty, the wonder, the divine essence came forth for all.

She felt the power of knowing radiating from the ever-growing multitude; now she was part of it. How long would it be before others would hear the call, and fly up to lend their love and warmth to bring forth a universal oneness?

From the rosy center of spirit egg, the gentle beating slowed. Robin Ray's body emitted a glowing brilliance. Her communion with spirit egg was complete. She was ready for a new journey.

In a dazzling explosion of light, the pure white beam reappeared. Robin watched enthralled as it slowly created a minuscule seed . . . a perfect seed of light, which then passed its light to a newly created one. The process was repeated over and over again. It is creation, Robin thought, expanding, continuous, everlasting . . . it is perfection . . . begetting . . . perfection!

Robin had learned well. She jumped up, her body glowing, and extended her shimmering wings.

I do remember, she thought. She took a long, deep breath, and then joyously shouted to the universe, "WE ARE ONE! . . . I AM THAT SEED!"

Then all was silent. She would remember no more.

In this sacred tranquility, the dulcet sounds of tiny bells resonated in perfect harmony. Robin Ray's body felt weightless. In moments, it was lustrously dissolving into minute points of light, all being swiftly drawn into the pure white beam, to become one with a now-forming perfect seed.

At the outer edge of the nest, softly clinging to a fine silver string woven of opalescent moonbeams, and formed by the all-loving creator of heaven and earth, was the seed of a new soul, now enshrined within a shining drop of dew.

As it descended slowly towards earth, its destiny below, it sparkled with unlimited potential.

A NEW BEGINNING

16

. . . a glorious morning

Robin Ray had no idea of why she had awakened lying on her back, firmly wedged in the low, sturdy fork of a tree. As the brightening pink morning sky began to illuminate its leaves, she lay wondering what had happened.

In a moment, looking upward, she recognized the familiar branches of her old nesting Oak and saw, securely straddling a higher limb, the nest that she and her mate had built. Instantly, Robin Ray flew upwards to find her startled mate sitting low on their nest, the eggs warm and safe under him.

"You're here! . . . you didn't leave us!" he cried in disbelief, quickly moving to the tree limb and settling close beside her. "I thought you were gone forever, Robin."

"I'm here . . . forever!" she replied softly, nestling under his outstretched wing.

Back in their nest, as an early-morning dew gently blanketed the old Oak, Robin noticed that a tiny Robin's bill had pierced one of her small blue eggs. She could hear a faint peep from the soon-to-be emerging baby chick.

Settling herself on the nest to nurture the new life and her three remaining eggs, she heard the clear call of a Mourning Dove. She looked down to the exact place in the garden where she had last seen her mother, recalling that sad day and the old woman who had honored her mother's passing with the spring-blooming lilac flower.

Then she turned her head to the back woods and thought about her father, and about her brothers' abrupt leaving – about how abandoned and alone she had felt.

It was a glorious spring morning. As she looked up and watched the sun moving higher, Robin Ray realized that somehow they would always be part of her. She would hold all of them in her memory . . . and would love them, and forgive them, as she would always forgive herself.

A few hours later, when she could feel a baby robin's wings moving under her warm body, she shifted her position. She could now see a little round head, with its yellow bill opened wide, trying to push up from beneath her pale red breast feathers.

The new-born, its eyes still closed, attempted to struggle to its feet, and his father, puffed with pride, declared, "He looks healthy and strong, doesn't he?"

"Indeed he does," Robin said.

Robin Ray knew that for every day to come, at last, she could now sing aloud for all to see her and to hear her song. She promised herself she would carol sweetly, with vibrant notes and melodies never before heard in that New England garden. After all, she thought, I AM ROBIN RAY, I AM A SONGBIRD, and this glorious morning is, truly, a new beginning.

Gazing at the familiar house and garden below, and then at her mate and their first baby chick, Robin murmured tenderly, "He is *perfect* – our new son is absolutely perfect!"

CODA

17

. . . renewing

It was after a particularly harsh early spring storm that had piled snowdrifts to the tops of the sills of the back porch windows that they had found the old woman inside her gray clapboard house.

She wore a robe of gray chenille over a white flannel nightgown. A black and white silk scarf was tucked in at her neck, and gray slippers on her feet. She sat erect in her favorite rocking chair, facing the old Oak tree and her beloved snow-covered garden, a pair of binoculars clasped tightly in her hands.

A red eiderdown comforter was pulled tight over her chest and tucked neatly under her frail arms. Her eyes were closed, and her lips slightly parted, as if she were about to speak.

A chilling late afternoon wind riffled her gray hair as two men, clad in black, carefully covered her lifeless body and moved it into a waiting black hearse.

As the long car moved slowly down the gravel driveway, the wind stopped. Behind, in silence, were the old Oak, the herb and flower gardens still asleep, the birdbath now frozen with ice, and the two bird feeders, which hung empty in the bitter-cold air.

When the hearse bearing this special soul had moved completely out of sight of the house, a brisk wind picked up again. The cold metal wind chimes on the back porch responded furiously, their sound carrying to the barren treetops.

On her perch atop the highest branch of the old Oak tree, alone, with her head facing into the wind, sat a very early, red-breasted returning migrant, a female American Robin. With bright eyes and her yellow bill opened wide, she was caroling sweetly, surveying her new territory, wondering where after the snow melted in this lovely garden she would build her spring nest.

Within the silent house, a sudden down-draft of wind through the brick chimney lifted the few papers on a small pine desk near the empty rocking chair, sending one piece floating to the wooden floor. There on the paper, in a firm but slightly faltering hand, the old woman had written:

If I shouldn't be alive
When the Robins come,
Give the one in Red Cravat,
A Memorial Crumb —

Emily Dickinson

THE NURTURERS

Sara Blackburn, my New York editor, first embraced the words, and then, with consummate understanding and care, deftly guided the weaving of the written threads into *The Nest*. Her generosity of spirit, her brilliance and perfect integrity will always be a part of this tale. What truly connects us to one another? Long ago, Sara knew the answer to this important question.

It is with a heart filled with love and pride that I express my deep gratitude for the inspired contributions to this book from my son, Robert Gleason Young, and my daughter, Susan Bryson Young. Their steadfast loyalty, rare humor, discerning taste and devoted nurturing of *The Nest* and of me embody the essence of loving family.

Jessie Gilmer read the first hand-written manuscript, strongly encouraged me to proceed, and kindly helped me to the next step.

Eleanor Kask Friede then graciously added her perceptive comments and insightful suggestions.

Eldon D. Greij, Ph.D., generously reviewed the manuscript for ornithological accuracy. He exemplifies the kindness and compassion of birders everywhere.

Kimball L. Garrett, Ornithology Collections Manager of the Natural History Museum of Los Angeles County, shared his erudition about birds' eggs and Central American hummingbirds.

I thank Congresswoman Mary Bono of the 44th Congressional District for her enthusiastic review of the segment on the Salton Sea, and also Nelda Linsk and Emma Santana of Palm Springs.

Jonathan Kirsch warmly shared his legal expertise and visionary spirit.

Judith Appelbaum kindly reviewed with me her publishing wisdom and caveats.

Doug Dutton was especially helpful with advice, as were Lise Friedman and Karen Wallace, also of Dutton's Brentwood Books.

C. E. Blevins expertly crafted exact replications of the book's birds' eggs, and Josie Castro-Young, my talented daughter-in-law, created the computer aspects of the website.

Early friends of *The Nest* include: Jacqueline Piatigorsky, Patty Lou and William Beaudine, Jr., Rodger E. Maus, Sam Wells, Jeanne and R. Richard Carens, Albert Van Court, Marcia McCall, Anna Padilla, Mimi and William N. MacGowan, Jr., Betsy Colwell, Wynnie Wynn, and B.T. and George Gallagher.

The Nest was inspired by the loving memory of my parents, Virginia and Robert Burns Morris, my sister Barb, wee Gram, Walter, Mabbie, my eldest son, Garth Morris Young, and the environmental pioneer, President Theodore Roosevelt.

It is written especially for the future guardians of our earth, including my three grandsons, Alex, Michael, and Maxwell, the youngest nestling, who makes my heart sing.

Ruby-throated Hummingbird
Archilochus colubris

American Robin
Turdus migratorius

Great Horned Owl
Bubo virginianus

Hermit Thrush
Catharus guttatus

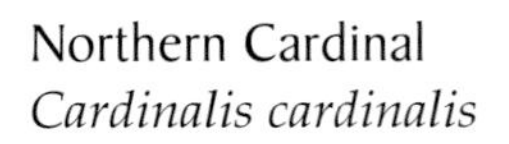

Northern Cardinal
Cardinalis cardinalis

Mourning Dove
Zenaida macroura

Sharp-shinned Hawk
Accipiter striatus

Resplendent Quetzal
Pharomachrus mocinno

Ruddy Duck
Oxyura jamaicensis

Shown at Actual Size

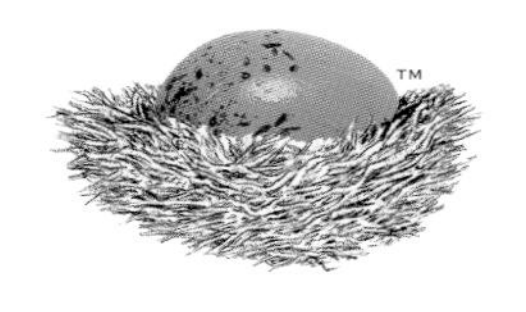

ARROWOOD BOOKS, INC.

2118 WILSHIRE BLVD., SUITE 271
SANTA MONICA, CALIFORNIA 90403

VISIT US AT OUR WEBSITE
WWW.ARROWOODBOOKS.COM